THE MECHANIC'S OBSESSION

A CURVY GIRL ALPHA MALE ROMANCE

ALPHA MALES LOVE CURVY GIRLS
BOOK ONE

KELSIE CALLOWAY

Kelsie
CALLOWAY
DARK, DIRTY, AND DANGEROUS ROMANCE

CONTENTS

1

AMELIA

I'm not exactly thrilled to still be living with my mother at 21, but desperate times call for desperate measures, and the truth is, I'm still figuring things out.

As I grab the lunch that she's packed for me, my eyes land on the sticky note she's left perched on top like a bright little flag. I'm sure she means for it to be positive and encouraging, but all I can read are the words dripping with condescension.

> Maybe you should walk to work this morning. It'll help you burn some calories!
> Love, Mom!

It's hard not to roll my eyes; I know that she means well, or at least I hope she does, but sometimes her actions don't come off in the best light. They feel more like reminders of my shortcomings rather than gestures of love.

With a sigh, I crumple up the sticky note, my fingers wrinkling it into a tiny ball before tossing it into the garbage can, a small act of defiance that feels oddly satisfying. I peer into the lunch bag, half-expecting to find the usual assortment of items. I've asked her a dozen times to stop packing a lunch for me, but no matter how many times I plead, she does it anyway. She insists that it's her way of showing me she cares, but I can't shake the feeling that there's an ulterior motive lurking beneath her good intentions. It feels like a subtle way for her to keep track of what I eat, a kind of surveillance disguised as maternal love.

Carrots, brown rice, and some grilled chicken. Oh, and another sticky note. I grab this one and toss it into the garbage with its twin, barely sparing it a glance. Mom's been trying to encourage me for years to lose weight, but at some point, she's got to wake up and realize that it's not as easy for me as it is for her. I could eat nothing but kale shakes for a year and still never reach her petite size 4. It's as if she's forgotten that bodies come in different shapes and sizes, each with its own set of challenges. I can almost hear her voice in my head, reminding me that "patience is key," but it feels more like a reminder of my shortcomings.

When I finally arrive at work, the first thing I see is Jameson flipping through a magazine that I left for him from yesterday's mail. His brow is furrowed in concentration, and I can't help but admire the way his dark hair falls slightly over his forehead. "Good morning," I greet him with a bright smile, trying to shake off the weight of my morning. "Did you see the marketing article I denoted for you?"

His eyes light up at my mention of the article, and I feel a small thrill at capturing his attention. As Jameson's Office Manager and de facto marketing guru, I'm always looking for ways to increase the profitability and sales of his mechanic shop. Although he only pays me to answer the phone, track his finances, and ensure that everyone in the shop gets paid every two weeks, I find myself constantly brainstorming new ideas in my free time. There's something satisfying about being a part of something bigger, a sense of purpose that goes beyond the daily grind. Plus, it's nice to feel like I'm contributing to his dream in some way, even if he doesn't always recognize it.

His dark blue eyes flick up from the glossy paper before him, and I feel my stomach churn at the intensity of his gaze as it locks onto mine. "I'm gonna be honest, honey, I didn't understand a word of what I read in that article. I get advertising, but they lost me with terms like ROI, A/B testing, and PPC online ads. I've got one job, and this," he emphasizes his point by slapping the magazine with his free hand, "ain't it, sweetheart."

The way he uses those terms of endearment used to make my heart flip over when I first started working for Jameson, igniting a flutter of excitement in my chest. But now, they've become part of the everyday rhythm of our interactions, comforting in their familiarity. He's twice my age, a fact that often weighs heavily on my mind, and he's never made a move on me despite the undeniable chemistry that crackles between us. I'm sure he's got more important things on his mind—like running the shop— and he definitely has a type that's blonder and tinier than I am. Yet, in those fleeting moments when the air thickens with unspoken tension, it's hard not to fantasize about what it would be like if a man who stands at an impressive 6'5" and is covered in tattoos would push me up against the door of the office and kiss me good and hard, and maybe a little bit more. It's a daydream that dances just out of reach, teasing me with possibilities that seem so far removed from our reality.

I clear my throat, striving to rid myself of those distracting thoughts before Jameson can sense them swirling in my expression. "That's what I'm here for. Give me a couple hundred dollars a month to play with, and in a few months, I can build up this business into—" But the frown etched on his face tells me he's already crunching the numbers in his head, and it seems he doesn't like the figures adding up. "Or not..."

"Amelia." His voice wraps around my name like a warning, sending a shiver racing down my spine. "I just don't know where we'll cut the costs."

If we hadn't had this conversation half a dozen times already, I would have tried to convince him that this investment would ultimately bring more money into the business. The adage 'you have to spend money to make money' holds a grain of truth, especially in this scenario. But instead, I simply let out a sigh, my shoulders drooping slightly, and nod my head in reluctant agreement.

I decide to shift the conversation, unwilling to dwell on a topic that's bound to upset us both. "So, what'd you do last night? Did you hit the bars?" I ask, hoping to draw him out of his brooding thoughts. On more than one occasion, he's stumbled into work with a raging hangover, his mood dark and heavy like storm clouds. He'll work in a broody silence, but you can always tell he's suffering from the night before. "I know you're a party animal, Jameson," I say, trying to coax him back into his usual playful mood, the banter that makes the long days at the shop more bearable.

"Not last night," he grins, his eyes sparkling with mischief, "but maybe tonight. You should come sometime. I think you'd enjoy it." Jameson follows me to the office, his presence warm and magnetic, as I ponder this unexpected invitation. The thought of spending the evening alongside him, away from the grease and oil of the shop, sends a flutter through my stomach.

Even though he's twice my age, I know that he can party harder than most of the twenty-one-year-olds

I know. I can imagine him effortlessly downing shots and laughing at the chaos around him, and I'm sure he'd drink me under the table without breaking a sweat. "I don't think that'd be wise. You're my boss and all," I reply, trying to keep my tone light, but the weight of the implications hangs heavy in the air. Besides that, if I get a little alcohol in me, I don't know what'll happen next—my mind races with possibilities, both thrilling and terrifying.

He takes a seat in one of the waiting area chairs, leaning back with a relaxed confidence that makes my heart skip a beat. "Who cares? Aren't you HR? Who are you going to report it to?" Jameson's never been one for rules, and I can't help but admire his defiance. Exhibit A: calling me pet names at work, which always leaves me blushing and flustered.

"The bar scene also isn't, well, my scene," I add, the words tumbling out of my mouth hesitantly as I look down at myself, hoping that he'll take the hint. I fidget with the hem of my shirt, acutely aware of my curves and how they don't quite fit the stereotype of the wild, carefree girl who flirts with strangers. "I'm not exactly the kind of girl who goes out to bars and gets looked at or talked to by the other guys. Not sure that's the environment for me."

My voice trails off, and I can't help but wonder if he sees me the way I wish he would or if I'm just another face in the crowd to him.

This time, I deliberately avoid making eye contact with Jameson. He's always been a nice guy, the kind who checks in on me and offers encouragement, but right now, I don't need him trying to father me with empty platitudes about how I'm beautiful no matter what size I am. I can't handle that kind of attention, especially not from him.

But he doesn't do that—not exactly. "What are you talking about, baby girl?" he asks, raising an eyebrow in that charming way of his. "You're gorgeous. Take it from a guy who knows a stunning woman when he sees her." His words hang in the air, and I can feel my cheeks heat up.

I feel my mouth dry up instantly as if the very air has been sucked out of the room. He's got to just be saying that to make me feel better, right? And, if I'm being honest with myself, *it's working!* A flutter of hope stirs within me. "Oh, um, Jameson," I stumble over my words, not quite sure how to respond to such unexpected praise.

He jumps to his feet, effortlessly exuding confidence, and sends me a wink along with that disarming smile that seems to light up the entire space. "I'll talk to you later, hot stuff," he says, his tone playful yet sincere. Then, just like that, he turns around and leaves the room as though nothing ever happened.

My heart is doing these pitter-patter-y things, racing in an erratic rhythm. I'm certain I've just dreamed up this entire scenario, my imagination running wild with the possibilities. But if I haven't, then what just happened? Did he really just call me gorgeous? The warmth spreads through me, mixing excitement with disbelief, leaving me both breathless and bewildered.

2

———

AMELIA

I'm knee-deep in my day, fingers flying over the keyboard, when Jameson strides over to me with a customer in tow. Normally, I'm the first face that people see when they walk through the shop's doors, welcoming them with a smile and a cheerful greeting. But somehow, this gentleman has managed to slip in through the back alley, his car in tow, and find his way to the owner of the company instead.

"Hey, Amelia," Jameson gruffly nods towards the guy, his voice a familiar rumble that always sends a flutter through me. "He'll be with you for about an hour or so. We're doing some repairs on his car. I'll get you all the info here in a little bit. The guys are doing an inspection right now to determine the full extent of the damage. Guess he got into a little fender bender."

I glance over at the man in question. He's only a couple of inches shorter than Jameson, but his presence is undeniably different. While Jameson is ruggedly handsome in his cut-off sleeves and dark gray mechanic pants, this gentleman is dressed far more professionally. A crisp button-up shirt is tucked neatly into tailored slacks, giving him an air of polished authority. "Well, take your time, sir," he says after a brief pause, casually waving Jameson off as if dismissing a minor inconvenience. "If I'd have known the receptionist was so sexy, I'd have come in sooner."

A blush creeps up my cheeks at his words, and I can't help but steal a glance at Jameson to see his reaction. His brow arches slightly, a subtle hint of amusement flickering in his eyes. I can feel the weight of the compliment hanging in the air between us, making the moment feel charged and a bit more complicated than it should be.

Jameson glares at the man with an intensity that makes my heart race, and then his gaze shifts to me, his expression fierce yet protective. "Watch yourself. We don't tolerate sexual harassment here." His voice is low but firm, the kind of tone that brooks no-nonsense.

"I'm Andrew," the man introduces himself as he steps closer to my desk, an easy smile playing on his lips. "And what might your name be, beautiful?" There's an air of confidence about him that both intrigues and unsettles me.

I open my mouth, ready to tell Jameson that it's fine, that I can handle this, but the sight of Jameson's clenched jaw and the telltale sign of steam practically radiating from his ears makes me hesitate. I suddenly feel as if I've entered an alternate universe. This man, who I've worked alongside for over a year, has just called me gorgeous, and now he's looking undeniably possessive over little old me, as if I'm a treasure he has no intention of sharing.

"Hey, dipshit." Jameson steps forward, closing the distance between himself and Andrew with a fierce determination that sends a flutter of excitement through me. He taps Andrew hard on the shoulder, a signal that's unmistakably serious. "Take your seat *over there*," he instructs, pointing towards the chairs at the other end of the office with an authority that brooks no debate. "And leave my Office Manager alone, or you can find yourself a new mechanic." His words are sharp, but there's a protective undertone that sends my heart soaring.

Andrew looks between me and Jameson, his hesitant smile faltering slightly. "Are you joking? Is this like, your girlfriend or something?" There's a hint of disbelief in his tone, and I can't help but feel a rush of warmth at the implication, even as the situation feels undeniably awkward.

I sit there frozen, my mind racing. Where my fight or flight reaction should kick in, I instead find myself caught in that third, often unspoken response: freeze. It's as if time has momentarily halted, leaving me suspended in this whirlwind of confusion and unexpected emotions.

"If she was my girlfriend, I'd have already kicked your ass. So sit down. Or else I'll kick it anyway." Jameson's voice is low and menacing, and I can feel the intensity of his glare slicing through the air. He crosses his arms over his chest, solid and imposing, giving Andrew a look that dares him to defy his orders. The protective energy radiating from

Jameson is palpable, and I can't help but feel a mix of admiration and trepidation.

I'm still sitting there, my thoughts swirling in a haze, wondering how everything spiraled into this moment. How did we go from casual conversations about car repairs to Jameson suddenly transforming from my boss into a possessive figure who seems ready to go to war on my behalf? It's bewildering, and I can't shake the flutter of hope that rises within me, even as the awkwardness of the situation lingers heavily in the air.

Andrew scoffs, a dismissive sound that drips with arrogance, but deep down, he knows he's no match for Jameson. Even though Andrew is nearly as tall as the mechanic, he can't compete with the sheer mass of muscle that Jameson possesses—at least fifty pounds of it. "Whatever. I don't have time for this pissing contest. She's a little too big for me anyway," he says, his words slicing through the air.

My heart sinks, and the initial shock begins to fade, replaced by a rush of indignation and hurt. The instinct to freeze in disbelief evaporates, and now my flight response kicks in. I stand up, my body moving almost on autopilot as I make my way toward the bathroom, desperate to escape the weight of the moment. But just before I can slip away, I hear Jameson's voice, firm and unwavering, telling Andrew to take his messed-up car and get out. The protective tone in his voice is meant to shield me, but it only heightens my emotional turmoil.

Before I even reach the bathroom door, I feel hot tears spilling down my cheeks, and I silently thank the universe that no one can see my vulnerability in this moment. Everything Jameson did for me this morning—his unwavering support and fierce protectiveness—feels utterly overshadowed by Andrew's cruel jab.

I've always known that I'm *a little too big* for men, and this interaction just serves as yet another reminder of that uncomfortable truth. It's a constant in my life, a reality I've learned to navigate like a tightrope walker, trying to maintain my balance while the world around me constantly shifts. Each time I'm confronted with this harsh reminder, it cuts a little deeper, a jagged edge that lingers long after the moment has passed. I try to tell myself that confidence is more important than size, but the sting of Andrew's words echoes in my mind, making it hard to believe.

I close the bathroom door behind me, leaning against it as I let the rest of the tears fall in peace, each drop a release of pent-up emotion. The small, tiled room feels like a sanctuary, a place where I can momentarily shield myself from judgment and the weight of the world. I take a deep breath, the cool air a stark contrast to the warmth of my cheeks, and I thank God again because Jameson doesn't come knocking to see if I'm okay. Maybe he knows I'm hurt and wants to give me my space, allowing me the time to gather my thoughts and regain my composure. Or perhaps, he understands that I wouldn't let him in anyway, that I'd keep my heart safely locked away, fearing what his concern might unveil.

He'd be right on both accounts.

JAMESON

I toss Andrew out of the shop, the sound of the door slamming behind him echoing in the otherwise quiet space, and I reluctantly bid farewell to what was probably upwards of $500 worth of repairs. I can already imagine the grumbling and frustration from the guys when they find out. It's going to be a tough sell trying to explain that it was all for Amelia. They wouldn't understand; they see the business in black and white, while I find myself tangled in shades of emotion when it comes to her.

The day I put out the ad for an Office Manager, I was in dire need of someone who could whip my disorganized office into shape. The last person I had in that role was a total schmuck who managed to screw everything up royally. I caught him embezzling money from the shop, and even though I took him to court, I never saw a damn penny of what he stole. The courts keep assuring me he'll pay it back, but it's all just empty promises, leaving me feeling even more frustrated with the whole situation.

Then Amelia walked through the doors, and everything changed. She was out of breath, her cheeks flushed, and I couldn't help but notice how her hair was a delightful mess, strands falling in chaotic waves around her face. Her story was that she'd walked from her place a mile and a half away, which only made me admire her determination even more. And then, in a funny twist of fate, she casually mentioned she was having car trouble herself. With a sparkle in her eye, she asked if, once she got the job, she could benefit from an employee discount. The way she said it, with a blend of hopefulness and charm, made it impossible for me not to smile.

She was beautiful. I nearly hired her on the spot, without even glancing at her resume. As she sat across from me, her eyes sparkling with enthusiasm, she tried to explain her situation. She didn't drop out of college because it was too hard; she simply didn't have the funds to finish her marketing degree. I felt for her, I truly did. I'd seen two or three other applicants who boasted more experience, but in the end, it was that gorgeous smile that completely disarmed me.

The first few weeks of training her were a challenge. I was still trying to wrap my head around the dynamics of the office, and she came bursting in with a whirlwind of ideas for our business. I often found myself having to tell her we didn't have the budget for her ambitious plans, and it pained me to see that beautiful face fall in disappointment. Yet, slowly but surely, she found her footing. As she grew more confident in her role, I couldn't help but notice how her energy transformed the atmosphere around her. I started coming in every morning not out of obligation to check her work, but simply because I wanted to see her, to talk to her, and to bask in the warmth of her presence.

I hate that she's only twenty-one. It gnaws at me, and I can't shake the feeling of being a pervert every time I catch myself looking at her, feeling a stirring between my thighs that I know I shouldn't. It makes the situation all the more complicated when I have to pull new hires aside and lay down the law: they can't touch her, look at her, or even think about her because she's mine. It's a possessive instinct that I can't quite explain, but it's there, deep-rooted and unyielding.

There's a running joke in the shop that I've claimed her, and while it's meant to be lighthearted, it carries a weight that I can't ignore. I might not have taken her to bed yet, but that's only because I assume she wouldn't be interested in an older man like me. She's too young, too vibrant, and too educated for a hardened mechanic like myself. I find myself wondering what she sees when she looks at me—if she sees the man I was or the one I am now, if she looks past the years etched into my face and the calluses on my hands.

Today, I took a chance, although it wasn't intentional at first. When I noticed the way her gaze dropped, filled with shame as she scrutinized herself, I felt a surge of protectiveness. I couldn't stand the thought of her thinking she wasn't beautiful. So, I stepped in, my voice firm yet gentle, determined to set her straight. I wanted her to see herself through my eyes, to recognize the radiance that I saw every time she walked into the room. When her cheeks flushed a delicate pink—what I hoped was delight—I felt a thrill of victory. But I left before I could be corrected, before the moment could slip away and turn into something I wasn't ready to face.

I sigh deeply, running a hand through my hair. The situation with Amelia has been messy, to say the least, and I knew that my friends wouldn't fully grasp the complexity of it all. They don't understand the connection that I have with Amelia, the way her eyes light up whenever she walks into the shop, the way her laughter makes my heart race.

"Jameson?" Jeremy's voice interrupts my thoughts. "You fixin' your hair for Amelia?" He asks, a smirk playing on his lips.

I roll my eyes, exasperated. "No, Jeremy," I say, my voice gruff. "I'm not fixin' my hair for Amelia. I'm just tired of dealing with assholes like Andrew."

He shrugs, clearly unconvinced. "Whatever you say, Jameson. Good luck catchin' your prey." He flips me off, mimicking my own gesture from earlier.

I let out a bitter laugh as I walk away. Jeremy doesn't understand what it means to care for someone, to want to protect them from the world's cruelty. He sees everything through the lens of a joke, but I know better. Amelia is more than just a pretty face or a good lay - she is someone who has stolen my heart and refuses to give it back.

4

JAMESON

Through the window, I can see that Amelia has returned to her desk, and I can't help but admire her once again. She looks as beautiful as ever, even though she's completely absorbed in her work. The familiar green and white colors of an Excel spreadsheet glow on her computer screen, but it's her that captivates me. She's wearing her reading glasses, which gives her an air of studiousness that I find utterly enchanting. In that moment, she reminds me of a naughty librarian, a fantasy I've indulged in more than once. The way her hair falls softly around her face as she leans in closer to the screen makes my heart race, and I can't shake the feeling that there's something more than just a professional connection between us.

As I enter the office, I felt a sense of calm wash over me. In this space, I could be myself, free from the judgmental eyes of the world. I hope that Amelia feels the same way, that she can find solace here as well. Because, at the end of the day, it isn't about catching my prey - it was about loving and being loved in return.

"Hey, sweetheart," I greet her warmly as I walk through the door, letting the familiar scent of oil and metal wrap around me like a comforting embrace. "I just want to apologize for what happened before. That should never have happened." I can feel the weight of my words hanging in the air between us, a fragile bridge to cross after the tension of the moment we shared. I hope she understands that my intentions were never meant to blur the lines of our professional relationship.

Amelia jumps at my sudden entrance, her surprise a mix of shock and charm that I find pretty cute. I can't help but smile at her reaction, the way her eyes widen and her breath catches for just a moment. "It's okay," I assure her, my tone gentle and reassuring. "It's not your fault." I want her to feel at ease, to know that the tension from before doesn't have to linger between us.

Well, naturally it's not Amelia's fault, but that doesn't mean I wouldn't happily lay into the guy who caused her such pain. The red rims around her eyes are a clear indicator that his cruel words have left a deep impact on her, and it takes all my self-control not to hunt him down and give him a piece of my mind. Or maybe something a bit more physical. It's a low blow for a man to say such things, and he doesn't deserve to get away with it.

"Amelia," I say, my voice steady and firm, "no man has the right to speak to you like that. It's not okay, and it's certainly not your fault. You deserve to be treated with respect and kindness, always." I can see the doubt and uncertainty in her eyes, and I hope that my words are enough to help her see that she's not to blame for someone else's cruelty. She's a strong, capable woman, and she deserves to be treated as such.

"No, really, Jameson, it's fine," Amelia tries to brush it off, but I can see the hurt in her eyes. I can't stand by and let her think that what that man said is acceptable.

I step towards her desk with a determined expression on my face. "It's not fine, Amelia," I say firmly. "You're beautiful, sexy, gorgeous, and the perfect size. Don't let what that man said make you feel like anything less. You're a smart, capable woman, and you deserve to be treated with respect and kindness, always. And you deserve to be loved for who you are, not for some idealized version of what someone else thinks you should be."

I can see the doubt and uncertainty in her eyes, but I also see a glimmer of hope. I hope that my words are enough to help her see that she's not to blame for someone else's cruelty. She's a strong, capable woman, and she deserves to be treated as such.

I take a deep breath and continue. "Amelia, I know that I'm not perfect. I'm an older man, and I own a mechanic shop. I'm not exactly the kind of guy that most women would look twice at. But I see you, and I see the amazing woman that you are. I see your strength, your intelligence, your kindness, and your beauty. And I want to be with you, Amelia. I want to be the one who treats you with the respect and love that you deserve."

I can see the surprise in her eyes, and I can tell that she's not used to hearing words like this. I hope that my words are enough to help her see that she's deserving of love and respect and that she doesn't have to settle for anything less.

I take a step closer to her and reach out to take her hand. "Amelia, will you give me a chance? Will you let me show you how much you mean to me?"

She looks up at me, and I can see the uncertainty in her eyes. But I can also see the hope, and the desire. And that's enough for me. I'll do whatever it takes to show her that she's worthy of love and respect, and that she deserves to be treated like the amazing woman that she is.

I can see her struggling to accept this. The wheels in her head are turning, and I can almost hear the gears grinding as she tries to solve a puzzle that seems impossibly tangled. I wish I could make her see what I see—the potential, the beauty, the strength within her that she often overlooks. "Stand up," I tell her, my voice steady and inviting.

She narrows her eyes at me, her expression a mix of suspicion and curiosity. "Why? What are you going to do?" The tension in the air is palpable, and I can sense her hesitation weighing heavily on both of us.

I've given her no reason to doubt me, yet I understand why she feels this way. After years of teasing and doubt, it's no wonder she's on guard, ready to protect herself from another disappointment. I can see the shadows of her past lingering in her eyes, and it makes my heart ache. "Nothing bad. Just stand up. Do you trust me?" My voice softens, hoping to break through the walls she's built around her heart.

Amelia huffs, her exasperation palpable as she pushes back in her chair. "No," she responds defiantly, yet I can see the wheels turning in her mind. "But I guess I have nothing to lose." With that, she stands up anyway, her determination mingling with uncertainty.

"Now come over here to me," I command, my voice firm and unyielding. The dominance in my tone is evident even to me, and I watch as a visible shiver runs down her spine. It's a small reaction, but it ignites something within me as she slowly follows my command, her steps hesitant yet deliberate.

"You know, there's only so many things you can get away with as my boss," she reminds me, a playful edge to her words. "There's a line somewhere and—"

Sometimes, she talks too much, and this is one of those times. The air between us thickens, and I decide it's time to take control. "Do us a favor," I cut her off, my tone brokering no argument, "and shut up."

Her mouth drops open in surprise as she stands in front of me, caught off guard. "Rude," Amelia whispers, her eyes narrowing slightly as she processes my words, "that's so rude." There's a spark there, a fire that I both admire and find utterly captivating.

Looking down at her, I can't help but smile. At 5'6", she's still almost a foot shorter than I am, yet there's an undeniable strength in her presence that makes her seem larger than life. "Your eyes are the color of honey, which is why I call you honey so much. It suits you, don't you think? And I call you sweetheart because you're the sweetest person I know, even more so than my mama. But I suppose that isn't a fair comparison; that woman is only five foot and she used to whoop my ass more times than I can count."

The laughter that escapes her lips fills the office, a warm and inviting sound that wraps around me like a cozy blanket. It lights up her face, and I can feel my heart swelling at the sight of her joy.

"That right there," I say, nodding towards her radiant smile, "when you laugh like that, you're simply radiant. You're the sun shining down on all of us, illuminating the shadows with your warmth. How do we dare to compare to someone as bright as you?" I watch her, hoping she understands just how special she truly is.

"I didn't know you were a poet, Jameson," Amelia says, a hint of surprise dancing in her eyes as she bites her lip, her cheeks flushing a delicate shade of pink.

I can't help but smile at her reaction, the way her body language shifts, revealing the vulnerability beneath her confident exterior. I reach out to grab her hands, feeling the warmth of her skin against mine, but I also notice that they're shaking just slightly. Yet, as I hold her hands firmly, they steady in my grip, and I can feel the connection between us deepening. "Amelia, I'm serious," I say, my voice low and sincere. "I don't know what you've been through in your life or who's made you feel like you're anything less than perfect, but you're beautiful. You need to hear this: pricks like that Andrew character aren't worth your time or your heart. He doesn't deserve your feelings or your tears or your time."

Her brow furrows as she processes my words, and she pauses, biting her lip harder as if she's weighing the weight of my honesty against her own insecurities. "I just, I don't think you should be talking to me this way," she finally responds, her voice tinged with uncertainty. "Maybe you should—"

It's been a year since Amelia walked into my life, and these feelings I've developed for her have steadily grown like a well-tended garden blossoming beneath the sun. It's not just the fact that she's beautiful, though she certainly is—a curvy woman with an infectious smile that lights up my dreary mechanic shop. It's also her sense of humor, the way she can make me laugh even on the longest, toughest days. She's kind and caring, always looking for ways to help my business thrive despite the fact that I can barely afford to pay her a fair wage. I know

I underpay her, and it eats at me; if I could find a way to invest in advertising or other improvements, I would prioritize giving her a raise first. She's not just an employee to me; she's transformed my office into a space I've always dreamed it could be.

I don't want Amelia simply because she's a captivating woman; it's her spirit that draws me in. I've grown to cherish the genuine connection we share, and even though I'm forty-two and she's much younger, I can't shake the feeling that there's something real between us. I hope that what I'm about to do doesn't scare her away.

"Shhh. Listen to me. You're perfect, Amelia. I promise." I lean down and press my lips to hers, feeling a rush of anticipation. It's my first real attempt to bridge the gap between us, to take that leap into a relationship I've longed for. Though she doesn't part her lips or kiss back in the way I had hoped, she doesn't immediately push me away either.

And that gives me hope. Hope that maybe, just maybe, she feels something, too.

5

AMELIA

My heart leaps into my throat when his lips land on mine, sending a shockwave of warmth coursing through my body. I want to pinch myself because I know that I must be dreaming. This can't be happening. It can't be real. A rush of disbelief mingles with exhilaration, making my head spin.

He smells of grease, a scent that has become so familiar from our long hours at the shop, mixed with the faint trace of whatever cologne he chose to wear this morning. That fragrance, now mingled with the essence of hard work and determination, clings to him, wrapping around me like a warm blanket. I want to fall into his embrace, to let go of all my worries and just be in this moment with him. But before I can succumb to that desire, I come to my senses and pull away, creating a painful distance that feels almost wrong.

"Jameson," I struggle to find the right words, my mind racing. How do I tell this sexy, older man that I'm not the right woman for him? The weight of my thoughts presses down on me, and I can feel the heat rising to my cheeks. He doesn't have to give me a pity kiss to make me feel better. He doesn't have to say all these sweet and wonderful things to rebuild my confidence. I'll be fine, really. I just need to convince myself of that before I lose my nerve completely.

I look up at him and see those beautiful blue eyes staring back at me. They're full of emotion, strength, and longing, a deep ocean of feelings that I can't quite decipher. I wish he was genuinely looking at me like this, without the weight of reality looming over us. "Jameson, you can't do this. We can't do this. You're my boss, you're twice my age, you don't really feel whatever *this* is for me."

The words hurt as they exit my mouth, like shards of glass cutting through the tender fabric of my heart. I can feel them tugging at the strings of my emotions, and I feel sick just saying them. My stomach churns violently, and for a split second, I wonder if I'm going to vomit right here in front of him. I've fantasized about Jameson kissing me since the day I started working for him, replaying those moments in my mind when the shop was quiet, but now that it's happened, it doesn't feel real. It feels like a dream I'm not ready to wake up from.

His grip on my hands tightens, grounding me in this moment. "What are you talking about, baby girl? None of that matters. None of that is true." His voice is low and soothing, but it only amplifies the storm within me. I want to believe him, to let go of my fears and insecurities, but the reality of our situation looms large and suffocating.

I can feel the tears already starting to build, a tightness in my throat threatening to spill over, and I try desperately to blink them back. "But it *does* matter," I say, my voice quivering slightly, betraying the turmoil brewing just beneath the surface. Please, God, don't let me cry in front of him. I can't bear the thought of showing him my vulnerability, especially when everything feels so precarious.

"Why?" His tone shifts, fierce and angry, echoing off the walls of the small shop. "Why does me being your boss matter? Who cares?" His words cut through the air like a blade, asserting his dominance in a way that both intimidates and captivates me. "If I met you at a bar and I wasn't your boss, I'd *still* be interested in you because you're gorgeous, Amelia." The sincerity in his voice is undeniable, but it only adds to my confusion. "I don't care if you're my employee. I don't think that makes you easy pickings or easy to manipulate or whatever." He leans in closer, as if trying to bridge the distance between our two worlds. "I think it makes it easier for me to come and chat with you when I'm bored or easier for me to ask you out, which I haven't done because I've been terrified you were going to say no, but I'm not afraid anymore. Because I think you feel for me exactly what I feel for you." His words hang heavy in the air, laden with a promise that both excites and terrifies me, igniting a flicker of hope amidst the storm of my doubts.

He can't possibly know what I feel for him. "You don't mean what you're saying, Jameson." My voice sounds even weaker than before, a mere whisper barely escaping my lips, because I'm overwhelmed by the whirlwind of emotions swirling inside me. Confusion clouds my thoughts as I grapple with the possibility that he might actually be sincere. What if he's being honest? The idea sends a shiver down my spine. "I'm not your type," I add, trying to convince myself more than him.

With a sudden, gentle yet firm movement, Jameson grabs my chin, tilting my face up to meet his intense gaze. "You most certainly are, sweetheart. You are perfect for me. I'm trying to make you see that." His words are a soothing balm to my insecurities, but they only amplify the storm raging within me.

I open my mouth to argue with him again, to throw out another self-deprecating remark, but he cuts me off before I can voice my doubts.

"If you put yourself down again, so help me God, Amelia, I will take you over my knee until you learn to see yourself through my eyes." The seriousness in his tone sends a jolt through me, my heart racing at the thought of his fierce determination. It's a strange mix of fear and exhilaration, and I can't help but wonder if he might actually be right.

I don't know if it's the threat or the authority behind his words, but a shiver of lust runs down my spine, igniting a fire I didn't expect to feel. I snap my mouth closed, the sudden silence between us thick with unspoken tension. The words that were previously at the tip of my tongue—those self-deprecating thoughts that had been my constant companions—get swallowed back down, and I decide they're better off left unsaid.

"As to your age, young lady," he begins in that same commanding tone, a timbre that feels both comforting and electrifying, "I hardly think that's a factor right now. You're brilliant. You can hold your own in a conversation with me, and honestly, I've seen you navigate far tougher discussions than most." His gaze locks onto mine, steady and unwavering, which only amplifies the fluttering in my chest. "It's not as though you're *under* age or anything, so I doubt we have anything to worry about. Unless you can't picture yourself with an older man, then I think this is a moot discussion we're having right now."

His words hang in the air, challenging me to confront my own reservations, and I can feel the weight of his gaze urging me to reconsider.

When he phrases it like that, he makes it hard to argue with him. His confidence is disarming, and I can feel my defenses crumbling.

"Do you have a problem with seeing an older man, Amelia?" He asks when I don't immediately respond, his voice steady, almost teasing, as if he knows the answer already.

I quickly shake my head no, my heart racing. The thought of him, of us, is both exhilarating and terrifying, and I can't help but feel the heat creeping up my cheeks.

"And as to my feelings," Jameson continues, addressing the last thing that I mentioned in my earlier tirade, "I think that all of this goes to show you that I do, indeed, have feelings for you." He pauses, his gaze unwavering, as if daring me to doubt him. "And if that's not clear enough, then let me be more frank. Ever since you walked through the front office doors to apply for this job, I've thought you were smart, funny, charming, and wildly beautiful." Each word feels like a gentle caress, wrapping around my heart. "Every day since, you have shown me that you're a kind and generous person, and I want to get to know who you are inside and out."

His sincerity washes over me like a warm wave, enveloping me in a sensation I've longed for but never thought I'd actually feel. For a moment, I'm completely lost in the depths of his eyes, those captivating pools that seem to hold a universe of emotion. In that gaze, I feel both seen and cherished, as if he can look right past my insecurities and into the very core of who I am.

I bite my lip, a futile attempt to stem the tide of emotions threatening to spill over. This time, though, I fight back tears not out of sadness, but from overwhelming joy and relief. All these months I've spent fantasizing about Jameson, weaving intricate daydreams in which he was mine while simultaneously telling myself it would never work out, only to realize now that he's been doing the same thing. The revelation fills me with a warmth that chases away the doubts I once clung to like a life raft in a stormy sea.

A shiver of excitement runs down my spine as Jameson's words hang in the air, enveloping me in their sincerity. I can't help but feel a flutter in my chest as I imagine the scenarios he's painted, each one more enticing than the last.

"I want to know what you're like on a Saturday night, when the week's worries have melted away and you let loose," he continues, his eyes sparkling with anticipation. "I want to see you dressed up and ready for a party, your hair cascading in soft curls and your smile radiant."

My heart skips a beat as I picture us standing side by side in the kitchen, laughing and cooking dinner together. The thought of sharing such a mundane yet intimate moment with him feels surprisingly comforting.

But it's his next words that truly take my breath away. "I want to see you undressed in the bedroom, on the verge of orgasm," he murmurs, his voice low and husky. I feel a blush creep up my cheeks at the boldness of his statement, but I can't deny the thrill that courses through me at the thought of being vulnerable with him in such a way.

Jameson takes a step closer, his fingers brushing against mine as he continues. "I want to dance with you at my favorite bar at 1:00 am, when the crowd has thinned and the music is just loud enough to drown out the world."

As he speaks, I can already feel the beat of the music pulsing through me, the thrill of being so close to him in the dimly lit room. And when he adds, "I want to experience life with you, Amelia, and see if we're meant to spend the rest of ours together," I know without a doubt that I want the same thing.

My heart starts pounding in my chest like a drum. The picture he's painting with his words is so beautiful, so vivid. It's a vision I've never imagined for us, nor one that I've ever really dared to dream up for myself. The idea that he feels this way about me is astonishing; I never thought I'd have any kind of future with someone as captivating as Jameson.

"Stay after work tonight," he says, a sly grin spreading across his face that makes my stomach flutter. "I want to talk to you some more, okay?"

I'm acutely aware that this moment, as perfect as it feels, eventually has to end. Yet, with the promise of more to come, I find that I don't even feel disappointed. In fact, I'm filled with an exhilarating sense of anticipation. "Yes, absolutely," I reply, my voice barely above a whisper, but the conviction behind it is unmistakable.

Jameson leans down to place a soft kiss on my forehead, and the warmth of his lips sends a delightful shiver through me. "I'll see you in a couple of hours," he says, his voice low and reassuring. Then, with a glance that lingers just a moment longer than necessary, he turns and strides toward the mechanic bay, ready to finish his work with an energy that makes my heart race.

I practically float back to my desk, lost in a dreamy haze of 'did that really just happen?' My mind buzzes with the thrill of it all, the reality of the moment washing over me like a wave. I can't believe that everything I've always wanted is really about to come true. A dominant, sexy, older man wants me. He thinks I'm beautiful just the way I am, and the thought sends a rush of warmth flooding my cheeks.

My mother has often said that this would happen one day, that I just had to get off my butt and work hard to get skinnier, but she would just die if she knew that it was happening now. That a man like Jameson—who owns his own business, who is successful and confident in his own right—was interested in little old me. Or, should I say, big old me. I can almost hear her voice echoing in my head, a mixture of disbelief and disbelief, but right now, that doesn't matter. What matters is that tonight, everything could change.

6

JAMESON

I attempt to clean myself up a few minutes after we close, but honestly, it's almost a futile effort. The rags I have on hand reek faintly of grease, so I'm essentially just smearing more grease over the spots I'm trying to wipe away. It's a messy battle, and I'm not even sure Amelia notices the effort I'm putting in, but I want to do right by her. I want her to see that I care.

When I finally mustered the courage to tell her how I truly felt, her face practically lit up with excitement. The way her eyes sparkled was something I'd never forget. Yet, beneath that joy, there was a flicker of fear, as if she was bracing herself for the moment I'd pull the rug out from under her and reveal that it was all just a prank. But deep down, I could tell that her excitement was genuine, and it made my heart race with hope.

When I hinted at the thought of her lying bare in my bedroom, teetering on the precipice of pleasure, the rosy hue that spread across her cheeks only served to fuel my own desire. I couldn't help but envision sweeping her off her feet and onto her desk, right then and there, to see if I could bring about that blissful release. And so, a part of the reason I asked her to remain after work was simply to explore this burgeoning connection. Perhaps it would blossom into a date, or perhaps something more intimate. Yet, Amelia's inscrutable demeanor left me guessing, and I found myself all the more intrigued by the mystery she presented.

I wanted to do right by her, to show her that my intentions were genuine. I wanted her to see the depth of my feelings and to trust in the potential of what we could share. That thrilling moment when she revealed her vulnerability, her fear of being hurt mixed with the unmistakable glimmer of hope, made me even more determined to protect her heart. I would be there for her, to catch her if she fell and to cherish her every step of the way.

As the evening wore on, I found myself drawn to her in a way I couldn't explain. Her laughter filled the room, as rich and warm as a summer breeze, and her eyes danced with a light that seemed to pierce right through me. I felt a connection with her that transcended the boundaries of our workplace, and I knew in that instant that I wanted to explore it further.

So, I took a chance and asked her out on a proper date. The way her face lit up at the prospect filled me with a sense of joy that I hadn't felt in ages. She agreed, and as we shared a smile that seemed to hold all the promise of the future, I couldn't help but feel grateful for the serendipitous twist of fate that had brought her into my life.

Together, we would navigate the complexities of our newfound relationship, learning to trust one another and to build a bond that would stand the test of time. And as I looked into her eyes, I knew that I would do everything in my power to make her happy, to be the man she deserved, and to cherish her always.

The men had all filtered out pretty quickly. They had other jobs, wives or girlfriends, or something else to get home to. So after getting as cleaned up as I was going to get, I hightailed it to the office where Amelia was still engulfed in work. She was no longer working on a spreadsheet, but her brunette locks were now piled high on her head in a clip as she scanned documents on her duplicate screens.

I let myself into the office, the familiar scent of paper and faint coffee lingering in the air. "Hey, gorgeous," I greet her with a smile that I hope conveys my affection before heading to the front doors to check if they're locked. With the city winding down outside, I want to ensure we have a little privacy. "Busy?"

She stands up, and I can see the nervous smile dancing on her lips—it's a mix of excitement and uncertainty about what's coming next. "I was staying that way while I waited for you," she replies, her voice steady but her eyes betraying a hint of curiosity. "So, what did you want to talk about, Jameson?" Amelia steps away from her desk and leans against the side, her arms crossed over her body, an unconscious barrier that I hope to break down.

Her crossed arms and guarded stance may scream "stay back," but I'm not about to let that deter me now. I've spent a year biding my time, waiting for the right moment to make my intentions known. My usual confidence took a back seat when it came to Amelia; I didn't want to risk our friendship or have her think I was some creepy older guy. But now that the cat's out of the bag and I know she feels the same, I'm not letting a little defensiveness stand between us.

With a nonchalant stride, I make my way across the room from the front door and close the distance between us. "So, I was hoping you'd given some more thought to what we talked about earlier. You know, the whole boyfriend-girlfriend thing, going on dates, sharing meals, sex, and... well, everything that comes with it." The words hang in the air as I watch her reaction closely, hoping she's on the same page as me.

Her face reddens at the mention of 'sex', and I can't help but grin even wider. I close the remaining distance between us, standing so close that I can feel the heat radiating off her body.

"Well, we'll have to keep things casual at work," she suggests, looking up at me with a mixture of defiance and vulnerability. "I don't want anyone here knowing about us."

I raise an eyebrow, trying to gauge whether she's serious or not. It's clear that the guys haven't been giving her a hard time like I initially thought, or else she would already be aware of their assumptions about us. "That's fine, but outside of these walls, you're mine, Amelia," I say firmly, watching as a visible shudder runs through her. "And I would want everyone to know it."

With that, I take the opportunity to close the gap between us completely, reaching out to take her hands in mine. She hesitates for a moment, her eyes searching mine, before finally allowing herself to relax into my touch. The tension between us seems to dissipate, replaced by a sense of excitement and anticipation for what's to come.

"Jameson, we can't do this here," she reminds me of the rule she just made, her voice a mix of playful protest and underlying thrill.

"No one is here," I whisper, leaning down to close the gap between us and kiss her. The warmth of her breath mingles with the cool air of the shop, heightening the tension that seems to hum around us.

Her mouth parts, ready to argue, but I seize the moment, slipping my tongue inside. Instead of a battle of words, our tongues dance with a fervent passion that has been building between us for far too long. Her hands release mine, finding their way around my neck, pulling me closer as if she can't get enough. I respond instinctively, grabbing her hips and lifting her effortlessly, setting her down on the desk with a sense of urgency and desire.

In a moment of fevered excitement, I bite gently on her bottom lip and growl, a primal urge surging through me. The sound that escapes her lips—a soft laugh—sends a rush of warmth through my veins, and I can't help but smile against her mouth, reveling in this intoxicating connection we share.

"You're an animal," she says, her voice barely above a whisper as she pulls away from me, her eyes sparkling with a mixture of amusement and desire. I can't help but grin at her teasing tone, my heart racing with excitement.

"I know what I want," I tell her, my lips curling into a smirk as I bypass her mouth and dive straight for her neck, kissing and nibbling on the sensitive spot just below her ear. I can feel her body trembling beneath my touch, her breath hitching in her throat as I reach for her jeans and begin to unbutton them. My own desire is palpable, my cock pressing against my pants, determined to make its own appearance.

"Lay down," I command, my voice low and husky with need. She looks behind her and pushes the stuff on her desk out of her way before doing as she's told, her eyes never leaving mine. I waste no time in removing her jeans and discarding them, leaving a pair of pink panties between me and my prize.

For a moment, I hesitate, my hand hovering over the delicate fabric. "Is it okay if I go further?" I ask her, my voice soft and gentle. She nods, her cheeks flushed with desire, and I can't resist the urge to kiss her again, my lips crushing against hers as I explore her body with my hands.

Amelia's agreement sends a wave of relief and excitement through me, and I silently offer a prayer of gratitude. I know I would have respected her decision if she had refused, but I can't deny the relief that washes over me at her consent. With a reverent touch, I hook my fingers into the waistband of her panties and slide them down her legs, savoring the feel of her soft skin against my fingertips. I can't help but let out a soft exclamation of appreciation as I take in the sight of her half-naked body, curvy and inviting. The desire to bring her pleasure consumes me, and I waste no time in positioning myself between her legs.

Amelia's thighs part easily for me, and I bury my face in the soft, fragrant folds of her sex. I hear her moan softly as I begin to explore her with my tongue, licking and teasing her sensitive nub with languorous strokes. The taste of her is intoxicating, and I find myself lost in the rhythm of pleasuring her. I slide a finger inside of her, feeling her warmth and wetness envelop me. Her hips buck up against me, and I hear her gasp as I curl my finger to find the spot that sets her off.

As I continue my exploration of Amelia's most intimate parts, I can't help but be captivated by the way her body responds to my touch. I flick her tiny nub a few times with my tongue, savoring the sound of her sharp intakes of breath and the swear words that escape her lips. I slide a second finger inside of her, adjusting my rhythm based on the motion of her hips and the urgency in her voice. Her stomach undulates beneath my hand, and I use it to hold her in place, trying to keep her still as the pleasure builds within her. Amelia grips my wrist tightly, our connection unbreakable, as she surrenders to the ecstasy that I'm providing her with. It's a powerful feeling, knowing that I have the ability to bring her such intense pleasure, and I'm determined to see her through to the end.

Her moans grow louder as I continue to lap at her, my tongue darting in and out of her folds as I savor the taste of her arousal. I slide three fingers inside of her, curling them upwards to hit her g-spot as I match the rhythm of her hips, which are now bucking wildly against my face. She gasps and moans, her breaths coming in short, ragged bursts as she approaches her climax.

"Fuck, Jameson," she cries out, her voice hoarse with pleasure. I can feel her muscles clenching around my fingers as she grinds herself against my face, chasing her release. The sounds of her pleasure are intoxicating, and I can feel myself growing harder with each passing second.

As her orgasm subsides, she collapses back onto the desk, her chest heaving as she tries to catch her breath. "Oh my god, that was amazing," she whispers, her voice still shaky.

I slowly withdraw my fingers from her, my movements gentle and deliberate. I discreetly wipe her juices off my face and kiss one of her thick thighs, which are still trembling slightly. "You're amazing, honey," I say, my voice low and husky. "One of a kind, actually." I can't help but feel like Amelia has ruined me for other women. No one else compares to her.

7

AMELIA

I haven't been with a lot of men. In fact, only two, and both of them were long-term boyfriends who never truly made me feel the way Jameson does. The fact that I just let him do *that* to me on my desk at work is still trying to sink in—my heart races at the thought. I can hardly believe I allowed myself to be so vulnerable, and yet here I am, feeling exhilarated and a little reckless. He's bringing me out of my shell in ways I didn't think were possible.

I sit up, brushing my hair back from my face, and look at him. He's leaning back in his chair with a look of satisfaction that practically radiates off him. He looks proud of himself, and honestly, who wouldn't be? In about five minutes, he took me from a nervous young woman unsure of her desires to someone who feels perfectly satisfied and alive. Of course, he's pleased with himself; how could he not be? "Your turn," I say with a grin that I can't contain because deep down, I'm a giver. He once told me that I'm kind and generous, and now, he's about to see just how generous I really am. The anticipation sends a thrill through me, and I can't wait to return the favor.

I hop off the desk, my heart racing with excitement, and nod towards my office chair, a playful glint in my eyes. "Take a seat, boss," I say with a wink, feeling a rush of empowerment as I invite him to let me take control for a moment.

"Amelia, you don't have to do this just because I—" He starts, the protest in his voice mixed with a hint of disbelief, but I can see the way his gaze lingers on me, caught between uncertainty and curiosity. The air between us crackles with a tension that feels almost electric, and I can't help but smile at the thought of what's about to unfold.

"I know," I interject, a playful smirk dancing on my lips. "But I want to." And it's true. I may not have much experience in this department, but there's something about Jameson that makes me eager to explore this with him.

His words about sharing experiences and possibly building a life together sparked a fire within me. It isn't just about the physical act; it's the emotional connection that truly turns me on. For men, it might be porn and visual stimuli, but for women like me, it's all about the emotional journey. The way he spoke about our future was intoxicating, and I want to do this for him right here and now.

"Are you sure?" he asks, his voice husky with desire.

I nod, a sultry smile spreading across my face. "Sit back, boss, and let me show you how much I want this, too."

As he settles into the chair, I can't help but feel a surge of empowerment. This was my chance to take control and show him just how much he means to me. And as I lean in, ready to explore this new side of our relationship, I know that tonight will be a night neither of us will ever forget.

"Take off your pants, Jameson," I command play-fully, adopting a mock-bossy attitude that makes my heart race with both excitement and a hint of mischief. "I said it's your turn."

He chuckles softly, the sound sending a thrill through me, and rolls his eyes in exaggerated disbelief. "If you say so. Maybe I should start calling *you* boss." But despite his teasing, I can see the spark of desire in his eyes as he complies. With a deliberate slowness, he removes his mechanic pants, the fabric sliding down his strong legs, and then he strips off his boxers. When his cock springs free, my breath catches in my throat, and I can't help but admire the sight before me. There's something undeniably empowering about taking the lead in this moment, and I relish every second of it.

As he settles into my office chair, I find myself sinking to my knees before him, my heart racing with a mix of excitement and nervousness. His impressive 7-inch cock is staring me in the face, and I can't help but wonder if I'll be able to handle it. But I'm determined to give it my all, to prove to Jameson that I can take control in the bedroom just as confidently as I can in the office.

I tentatively reach out and wrap one hand around his cock, marveling at the contrast between the soft skin and the rock-hard shaft beneath it. I begin to stroke him slowly, savoring the feel of him in my grip and the way his breath hitches in response.

"Damn, you already feel good," he murmurs, his voice low and husky. The words send a thrill through me, and I redouble my efforts, eager to pleasure him and to take advantage of this rare moment of vulnerability from my usually confident and commanding boss.

I wrap both hands around his cock, the throb of his arousal pulsing against my palms. A fantasy flashes through my mind, of him sweeping me off my feet, throwing me onto the desk, and taking me with an urgency that leaves me breathless. I bite my lip, suppressing the urge to tell him that I've reconsidered, that I want him to do just that. Instead, I focus on pleasuring him with my mouth.

I lean down, parting my lips to take him in. He's too big for me to take more than a few inches without hitting the back of my throat, but I don't let that deter me. I pull back, using my saliva to lubricate him before swirling my tongue around the tip of his cock. He groans, his hips bucking slightly as I lick him like a melting ice cream cone. My hands work in tandem with my mouth, stroking him with firm, deliberate movements as I savor the taste of him.

I give him a nod, silently communicating my understanding. "Don't hold back," I whisper, my voice barely audible. "I want you to use my mouth however you want."

With a sense of determination, I take him back in, feeling him hit the back of my throat once again. This time, Jameson doesn't hold back. He thrusts deeper, causing me to gag slightly, but I refuse to back down. I relax my throat and take him in, feeling the head of his cock hit the back of my throat.

Tears start to well up in my eyes as he continues to fuck my mouth, but I don't stop. I savor the feeling of him using me like this, the taste of him on my tongue, and the sounds of his pleasure filling the room.

Suddenly, Jameson pulls back, his breath heavy. "Fuck, Amelia," he says, his voice strained. "We need to stop."

I pull back, wiping my mouth with the back of my hand. "What? Did I do something wrong?"

His eyes look raw and wild, full of lust. "I have to fuck you. I'm not cumming in your mouth." He grabs me by the arms and helps me to my feet." He grabs the hem of my shirt and pulls it over my head. "God, you're beautiful."

I instinctively cover my stomach, a habit I've developed over the years. Standing before him, nearly naked, I can't help but feel self-conscious. "Jameson, stop."

But he doesn't listen. Instead, he insists, "No, Amelia, you stop. You're gorgeous."

I try to protest, pointing out the areas I'm most insecure about. "I'm not though. I need to lose weight here, here, and here," I say, gesturing towards my thighs, stomach, and breasts.

But Jameson doesn't give me a chance to continue. He quickly turns me around so I'm facing the desk and bends me over it without warning.

"What are you doing?" I ask, my voice shaking.

"I already warned you what would happen if you continued to put yourself down," he says matter-of-factly, his voice stern yet tinged with concern. Before

I can even register what's happening, he brings his hand down on my bare bottom with a sharp smack.

"Hey!" I cry out in surprise, my body tensing as I feel the sting radiate across my sensitive skin. I squirm and try to wriggle away from his grasp, but he holds me firmly in place, his other hand gripping my hip. "Stop that! You can't just...do that!"

But Jameson doesn't listen. He continues to rain down swats on my bottom, alternating between each cheek. I shift my weight from foot to foot, trying to dance my way out of his reach, but it's no use. The smacks keep coming, each one harder than the last.

"Jameson, please! That hurts!" I plead, my voice trembling as I try to fight back tears. But he doesn't relent. Instead, he keeps spanking me, covering every inch of my bottom with a fiery heat.

"What hurts is that you can't see how beautiful you are to me," he says over the sound of his hand meeting my flesh. "What hurts is that you're questioning my judgment every time I tell you that you're gorgeous, and you tell me no."

I bite my lip, trying to hold back a sob. I know he's right, but it's hard to believe him when all I can see are my flaws. Still, as I feel his hand caress my sore bottom, I can't help but feel a small flicker of hope. Maybe, just maybe, he sees something in me that I don't.

My bottom feels like it's been set ablaze, and I can feel the hot tears welling up in my eyes. "I'm sorry, Jameson, I truly am," I manage to say, my voice quivering. "I don't want to feel this way about myself."

Jameson stops his swats, and I feel his strong arms encircle my waist from behind. "I know it's not going to be easy to change a lifetime of negative self-talk, sweetheart," he says gently, "but the first step is going to be accepting when I tell you that I think you're beautiful. Can you understand that?"

I sniffle a little, wincing as my sore bottom throbs. But I nod my head, feeling a small sense of resolve beginning to build within me. Somewhere deep inside, I feel a strange mix of emotions - the sting of Jameson's hand on my flesh, the tenderness of his embrace, and the confusing realization that I'm somehow turned on by all of this.

"Jameson," I say hesitantly, "would it be weird if we... you know, still had sex?"

He chuckles softly and spins me around, dipping his head to capture my lips in a tender kiss. "I was really hoping you'd say that," he murmurs, the warmth of his breath sending a shiver down my spine. He skillfully unhooks my bra, freeing my breasts from their confines. "God, you're exquisite. Don't ever hide yourself from me again. You're only depriving both of us when you do."

I can feel my cheeks flushing with embarrassment, and the urge to shield myself with my arms is almost overwhelming. But the lingering sting of his hand on my bottom serves as a potent deterrent, and I force myself to keep my hands at my sides. I offer him a timid smile instead, watching as he eagerly buries his face in my cleavage.

"I want to adore every inch of this gorgeous body for the rest of my existence," he growls, the raw desire in his voice making my heart race. I close my eyes and lean into him, feeling a surge of pleasure at the thought of being his forever.

And I want him to, too. I turn around and lean over the desk again, this time willingly, my curves pressed against the cold wooden surface. I take a deep breath and whisper, "I want you, Jameson." I wanted to tell him to fuck me, but I wasn't quite brave enough yet. Maybe next time.

His responding growl is low and deep, sending a shiver down my spine. "My pleasure, baby girl, and hopefully yours, too." He steps forward, and I can feel the tip of his cock teasing at my entrance for just a few seconds before it plunges deep inside my pussy.

For a moment, he stills, giving me a chance to adjust to his size. I bite my lip, trying to hold back the moan that threatens to escape. Once I'm ready, he begins to move, pumping in and out with excruciating slowness. At first, I think he's doing it to make sure that I can handle him, but after a minute of this, I realize that he's teasing me. I swivel my hips, trying to convince him to speed up, but he just keeps up at his punishingly slow pace. "Jameson," I say warningly, my voice strained with desire.

"Yes?" he asks, his voice low and gravelly.

I can barely get the words out, I'm so overwhelmed by the sensation of him inside me. "Fuck. Me. Harder."

That's all it takes to get his engine revving. He slams into me, and even though my hips hit the desk, it's the best pain I've felt in a while. I swear under my breath as he picks up his pace, a glorious, earth-shattering fucking that I haven't felt in my entire life. Those two ex-boyfriends that I had sex with have nothing on Jameson.

He stretches my pussy to its limits, holding onto my waist as he pounds into me just as I requested. "You agree to be mine, Amelia?" He asks with each stroke of his cock, his voice strained with effort.

I can't think straight, but I know that I want this. I want him. "Yes," I moan, my voice breaking with desire. "I'm yours, Jameson. All yours."

He growls in response, his movements becoming even more frenzied as he chases his release.

I'm lost in a haze of pleasure, my thoughts scattered like leaves in the wind. Jameson's cock stretches me to my limits, filling me completely as he pounds into me with a fervor that takes my breath away. I can't help but moan and push back against him, desperate for more.

"Fuck, yes," I cry out, my voice ragged with desire. He could have asked me to do anything in this moment, and I would have agreed without hesitation.

But Jameson isn't content to simply ravish me. He wants to make sure I'm fully committed to him, that I'll do whatever it takes to please him. "You'll learn to love your body in all its glory?" he asks, his voice strained with effort.

I wish he would stop asking questions and just focus on the pleasure, but I know what he's doing. He's using sex to manipulate me, to bend me to his will. And damn it, it's working. "God damn it, yes," I manage to choke out.

Jameson seems pleased with my answer, his movements becoming even more frenzied. "Good," he growls. "Because every time you don't, you're getting another spanking." I shiver at the thought, both terrified and turned on by the prospect. But I know that I'll do anything to avoid that punishment, to keep Jameson happy and satisfied.

Joke's on him, because even though it stung and left me momentarily breathless, it also kindled a fire within me. But he doesn't need to know that. With a smirk, I retort, "You talk too much."

His response is immediate and startling, a sharp smack on my backside that sends a jolt of electric pleasure coursing through my body. God, he's perfect. I never knew that this was what I craved in a partner until it was happening right before my eyes.

Jameson's fingers dig into my waist, holding me tightly as his own pleasure builds. I can feel the tension coiling within him, and it only serves to heighten my own arousal. "You're gonna make me cum, baby girl," he growls in my ear, his voice low and rough. And I know that I'll do anything to make that happen.

The unexpected sensation does something to me. My body responds with an intensity I've never experienced before. My pussy clenches, and I arch my back, crying out in pleasure as I have my second orgasm of the day. Jameson's fingers dig deeper into my waist, holding me tightly as his own pleasure builds. He leans into me, his hard body pressed against mine as he roars my name.

I never could have predicted that this is how my day would end. Earlier, I imagined going home to my mom and thanking her for the vegetables and low-calorie lunch she packed for me. I would apologize for not walking to work and promise to do better tomorrow. We would talk about my options for a gym membership for the new year, but I knew I would either forget or never use it.

But instead, I had an encounter with a rude customer that led to the best experience of my life. As Jameson passes me my panties, his cum dripping down my thighs, I can't help but think that my entire life has changed today. And it's only going to get better from here.

"We probably did this in the wrong order," Jameson says, an embarrassed smile creeping across his handsome face, his charming eyes sparkling with mischief. "Because I still don't have your number, your address, or even know when we're going to have our first date."

I pull on my jeans, the fabric soft against my skin, and laugh, fully aware that he's absolutely right. This isn't exactly the story I envision telling our kids one day—at least not in the beginning. "Well, I guess we'll have to remedy that, now won't we?" I tease, enjoying the flirtation that dances between us.

He looks as happy as I feel, his grin infectious and bright. "You're perfect, Amelia. And you're finally mine. Just tell me what to do next and I'll do it," he says, his voice low and sincere, sending a thrill through me.

"Well, I wouldn't mind getting a quick dinner if you're up for it," I suggest, my stomach growling softly, a reminder of how famished I suddenly feel. "I'm famished for some reason."

"Couldn't have been those two orgasms," he replies nonchalantly, a teasing twinkle in his eyes. "Probably the busy workday."

I pull on my shirt, the fabric settling comfortably around me, and nod in agreement, a smile still playing on my lips. "Must have been," I say, feeling a warmth blooming in my chest, knowing that this is just the beginning of something exceptional.

ALSO BY KELSIE CALLOWAY

For more books...

Check out my Amazon page:

https://geni.us/KelsieCallowayAmz

Check out my website:

https://geni.us/KelsieCalloway

HAVE YOU LEFT A REVIEW?

Reviews are an author's bread and butter. This is how new readers find us and how old readers determine if a new series is worth their time. If you enjoyed this book, take a moment to leave a review or put in a recommendation on BookBub.

Scan with your phone camera!